NOT A FOX

by Arthur Strangekin

3965904

This book is dedicated to you, Ma.
Thank you and I love you.

First Edition
Published by Strangekin Press
www.Strangekinpress.com
ISBN: 978-1-77630-230-7

... with a delicious master plan!

Excuse me, Sir. I am a chicken scientist.
May I borrow a chicken for . . .
er . . research, please?

Hmmm. . . . Are you *sure* you're a scientist?
Your ears seem quite pointy.

Of course I'm a scientist!
Look at my glasses. Look at my clipboard!

Ah yes, you *do* look clever.
Very well. You can borrow Minnie.

Plan B : Fowl Play
Police hat
sunglasses
cool pose
muscles
BOOM!!
obeys my authority
explosions
Kapow!!
add
Spice
carrots
mushrooms
onions

. . . there's space in the pot for *one* more.

Hello, kind stranger! I couldn't help but
notice your magnificent chicken! I, myself, am in
the market for a chicken. Would you perhaps be
willing to sell her for a large lump sum?

Wait a minute. Are you *sure* you're not that
chicken-scientist-police-person-fox in a new disguise?

How dare you, Sir!? A fox, you say? Nay!
I am but a humble businessman.

Yes, well. A large lump sum *would* be quite handy.
Very well. I will sell you Margo. Take good care of her.

Rustle

GRRR

Rustle. Rustle

WOOF
WOOF
WOOF

Eeeeeeeeeeee

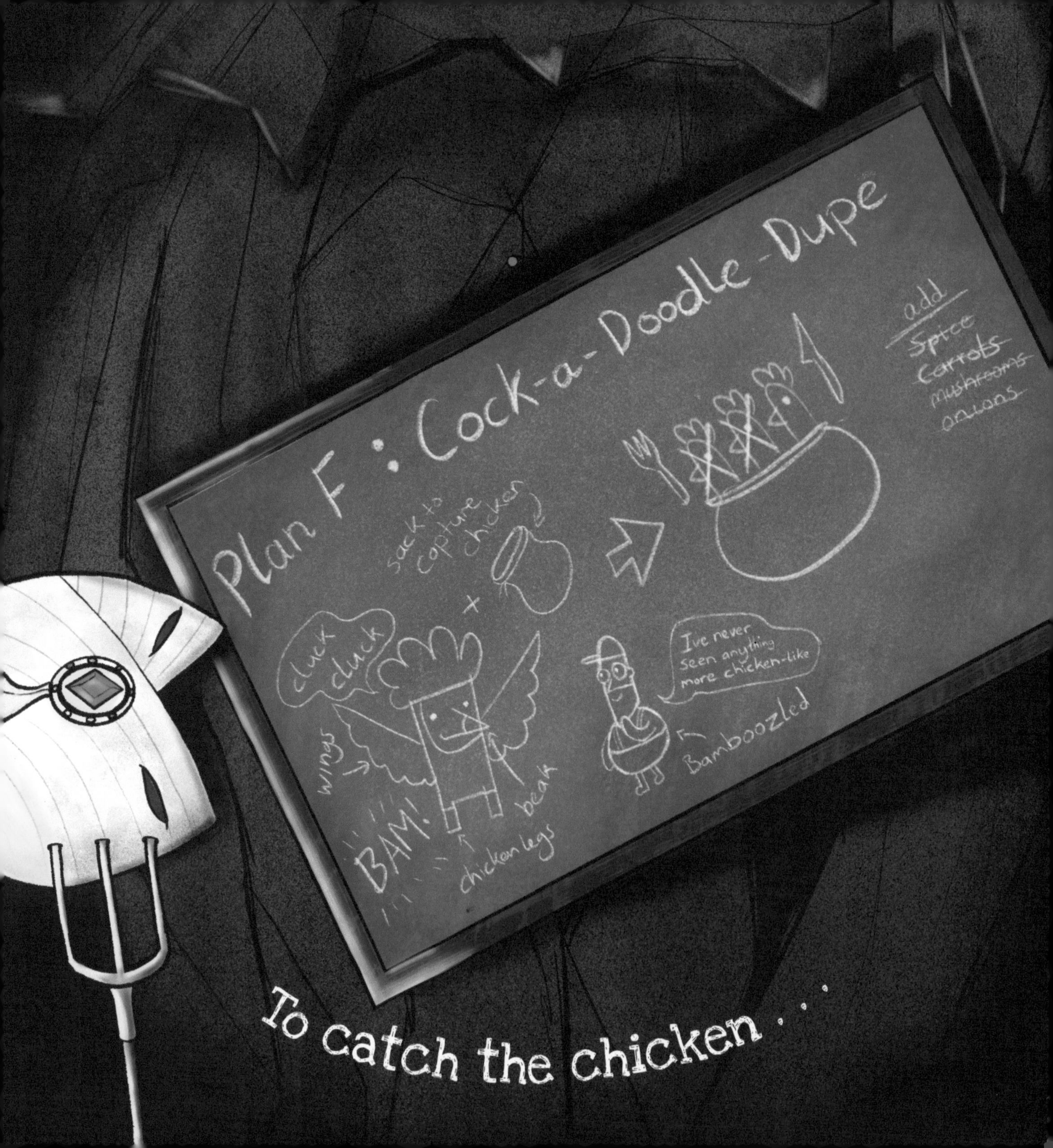

To catch the chicken . . .

Cluck

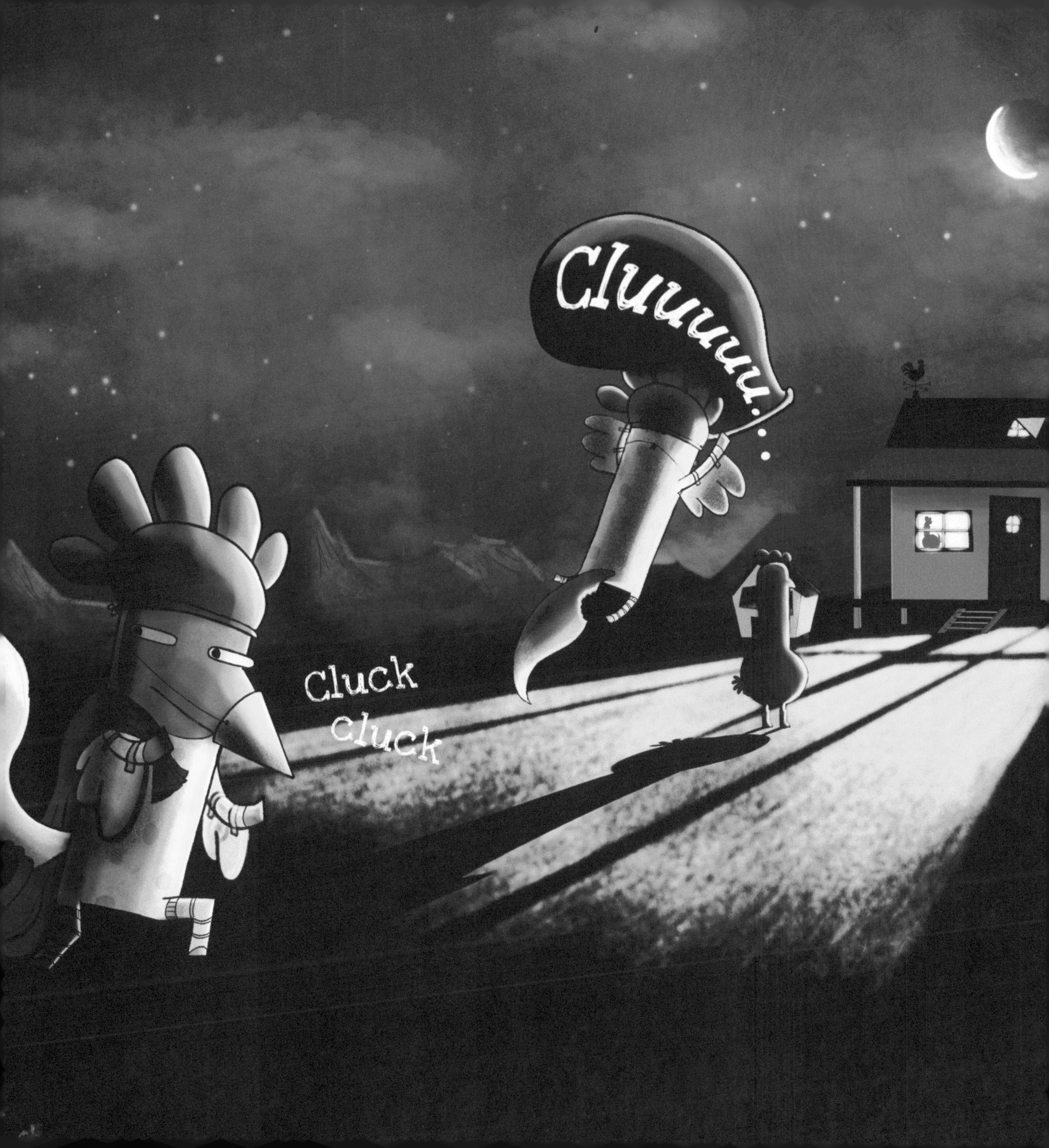
Cluuuuuu...
Cluck cluck

wait a minute,
you're . . .

. . . not a
chicken.

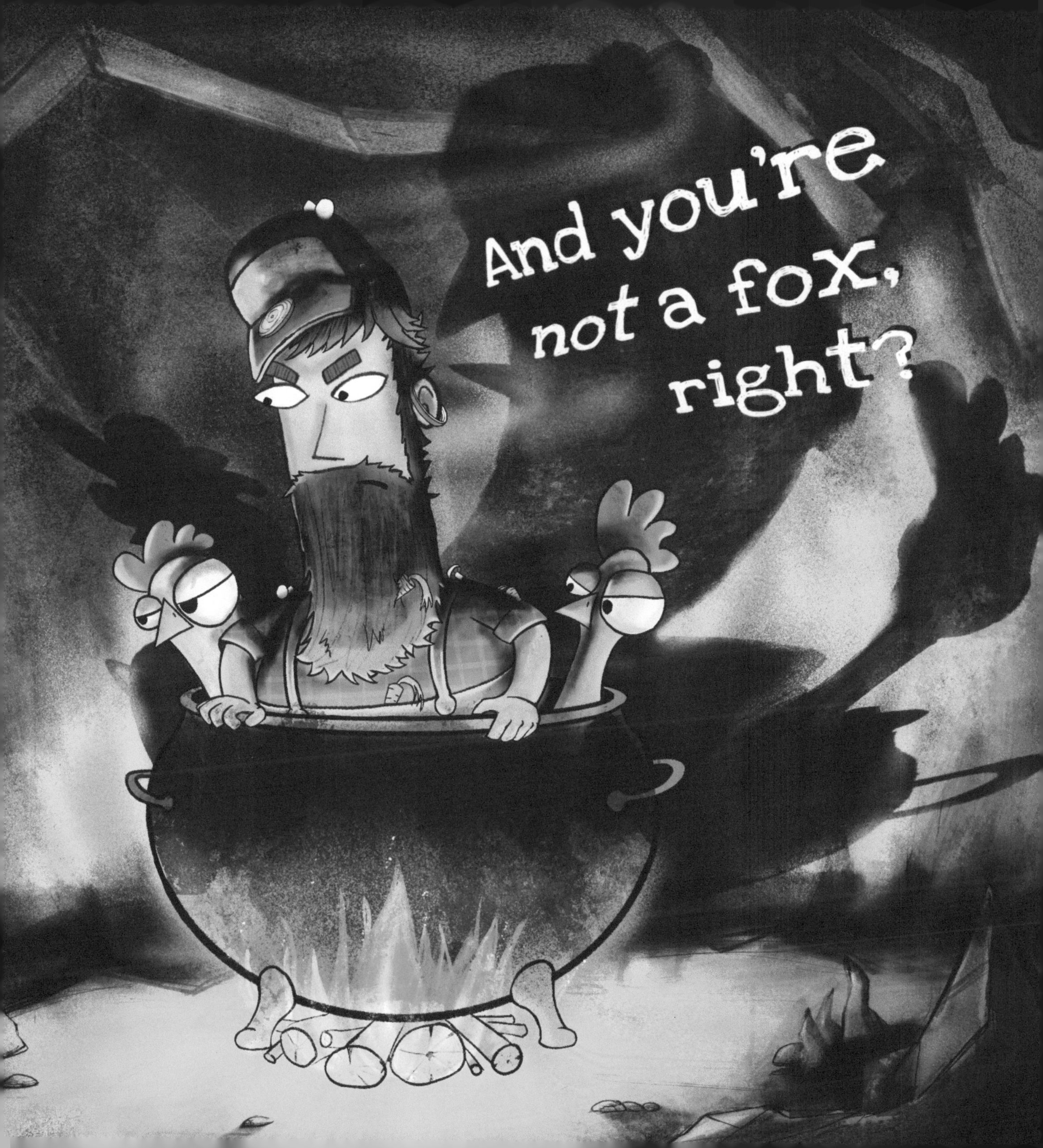
And you're not a fox, right?

The end.

CPSIA information can be obtained
at www.ICGtesting.com
Printed in the USA
BVHW021520210521
607789BV00002B/38